Best Friends

Anna Michaels
Illustrated by G. Brian Karas

Green Light Readers
Harcourt, Inc.

Orlando Austin New York San Diego Toronto London

Chapter 1
Apple Snack

Pick one.
Pick two.

Pick for me.
Pick for you.

Pick this.
Pick that.

One in my cap.
Two in your hat.

All done.
Let's go, Zack.

Wait, Dan.
One more to pack.

Sit, Nick!
Sit, Mack!

It is time for our apple snack.

Think About It

1. Is "Apple Snack" a good title for this story? Why or why not?

2. Who ate the apple snack?

3. How might the story have been different if Dan and Zack had other pets, such as fish or birds?

4. What is your favorite snack?

Chapter 2
What Is It?

I have a surprise.

What is it, Dan?
Is it big?

It is not big.

What is it, Dan?
Is it in your hand?

It is not in my hand.

What is it, Dan?
Is it in the yard?

Here it is.

It is a snail.

What a surprise!

Think About It

1. What do Dan's clues tell you about the surprise?

2. How do the words and pictures help to tell the story?

3. Why do you think Dan wants to surprise Zack?

4. Would you have liked Dan's surprise? Why or why not?

HERE COMES THE SUN

Dan and Zack like to pick apples.

Make a mural to show what you like
to do on sunny days.

mural paper **paints** **brushes**

1. Paint pictures of what you like to do when the sun is out.

2. Is today a sunny day? Choose something from your mural to do outdoors.

Make a book showing what you like about a special friend!

WHAT YOU'LL NEED

paper   crayons or markers   stapler

1.

Fold two pieces of paper in half. Staple them together.

2.

Make a cover for your book.

3.

On each page, write one thing your friend can do. Draw a picture about it.

After you make your book, give it to your special friend. Then you can read it together!

Meet the Illustrator

G. Brian Karas used to be a greeting card artist, but he likes writing and illustrating books even better. Now he gets to go to schools and talk to kids about his work. And his two sons give him lots of ideas for characters. He hopes that your friends and family give you story ideas, too!

www.HarcourtBooks.com

First Green Light Readers edition 2004
Green Light Readers is a trademark of Harcourt, Inc., registered in the United States of America and/or other jurisdictions.

Library of Congress Cataloging-in-Publication Data
Michaels, Anna.
Best friends/Anna Michaels; illustrated by G. Brian Karas.
p. cm.
"Green Light Readers."
Summary: Best friends Dan and Zack pick apples and find a snail in the garden.
[1. Best friends—Fiction.] I. Karas, G. Brian, ill. II. Title.
III. Series: Green Light Reader.
PZ7.M58115Be 2004
[E]—dc22N 2003017413
ISBN 0-15-205136-8
ISBN 0-15-205133-3 pb

C E G H F D B
C E G H F D B (pb)

Ages 4-6
Grade: 1
Guided Reading Level: E
Reading Recovery Level: 7

Green Light Readers
For the reader who's ready to GO!

"A must-have for any family with a beginning reader."—*Boston Sunday Herald*

"You can't go wrong with adding several copies of these terrific books to your beginning-to-read collection."—*School Library Journal*

"A winner for the beginner."—*Booklist*

Five Tips to Help Your Child Become a Great Reader

1. Get involved. Reading aloud to and with your child is just as important as encouraging your child to read independently.

2. Be curious. Ask questions about what your child is reading.

3. Make reading fun. Allow your child to pick books on subjects that interest her or him.

4. Words are everywhere—not just in books. Practice reading signs, packages, and cereal boxes with your child.

5. Set a good example. Make sure your child sees YOU reading.

Why Green Light Readers Is the Best Series for Your New Reader

- Created exclusively for beginning readers by some of the biggest and brightest names in children's books

- Reinforces the reading skills your child is learning in school

- Encourages children to read—and finish—books by themselves

- Offers extra enrichment through fun, age-appropriate activities unique to each story

- Incorporates characteristics of the Reading Recovery program used by educators

- Developed with Harcourt School Publishers and credentialed educational consultants